This is for Eric, and for
all the smiles this will bring you.
—K.S.

Library of Congress Cataloging in Publication Number: 2015940010

ISBN: 978-1-59474-858-5

Printed in China

Typeset in Clarendon and VAG Rounded

Designed by Timothy O'Donnell
Text adapted by Jason Rekulak, Rick Chillot, and Blair Thornburgh
Special thanks to Josh Izzo and Joanna Cotler
Production management by John J. McGurk

Quirk Books
215 Church Street
Philadelphia, PA 19106
quirkbooks.com

10 9 8 7 6 5 4

HOME ALONE

The Classic Illustrated Storybook

Based on the story written by John Hughes
and directed by Chris Columbus
Illustrated by Kim Smith

QUIRK BOOKS

PHILADELPHIA

'Twas three nights before Christmas,
and the McCallister family was getting
ready to leave for vacation.

Everyone was busy packing.

Everyone except Kevin,
who was busy getting
into trouble.

"Go straight to bed!"
his mother demanded.
"That's enough trouble
for one day!"

Lying in bed, Kevin could hear voices
and laughter coming from downstairs.
Everyone was having fun without him.

"I hope I never see my family again,"
Kevin whispered.
"I wish I was home alone."

The next morning, the house
was very, very quiet.

No one was shouting. No one was running
around. No one was telling Kevin to hurry up
and eat his breakfast. No one was home.

Finally, Kevin realized what had happened.

For the first time ever,
Kevin had the house
all to himself.

He ~~raced~~ up and down
the halls.

He jumped on all the beds.

He ate a **giant** ice cream
sundae for breakfast.

After watching hours
of television,

he searched through his
brother's private stuff

and
rode
a
toboggan
down
a
giant
mountain.

AHHHHHHH!!!

He even tried his father's
after-shave lotion.
(This was not a good idea—
it stings!)

But sometimes it was scary to be all alone.

Kevin was especially afraid of his next-door neighbor. Old Man Marley was the scariest person who lived on their block.

And that night Kevin heard whispers outside the living room window. Burglars were snooping around his house!

"You see?" Marv said. "Most of the houses on this street are empty! Everyone is away for the holidays!"

"Perfect," Harry said. "We'll come back tomorrow night and steal everything!"

Kevin was so scared, he dialed 911,
but the telephone didn't work.
The wires had been damaged in a snowstorm.

After hiding under his parents' bed for a long
time, Kevin decided that he was being silly.

"Only a wimp would be hiding, and I can't
be a wimp. I'm the grown-up of this house,
and I need to act like one!"

The next day was Christmas Eve, and Kevin had plenty of grown-up work to do.

He walked to the grocery store and bought food.

He put his clothes in the washing machine.

He decorated a Christmas tree.

And he hung Christmas stockings for his parents and brothers and sisters.

"I miss you guys," he whispered. "I wish you would come back."

Kevin's family always went to church on Christmas Eve, so that's what Kevin did, too.

After the service ended, he saw his scary next-door neighbor, Old Man Marley, sitting nearby.

"You don't have to be afraid," Mr. Marley
said. "The kids in the neighborhood
have lots of spooky stories about me,
but they're not true."

After they talked for a while,
Kevin realized that Mr. Marley was
in fact a very nice man.

"Are you visiting anyone for Christmas?"
Kevin asked.

"No," Mr. Marley said.
"I miss my family and I'd like to
see them, but my son and I are
fighting. I said some angry words
that I didn't mean."

Kevin knew exactly how
Mr. Marley felt.

Kevin remembered wishing
his family would disappear—
but he hadn't really meant it.

"You should try talking
to your son," Kevin said.
"Maybe I will," Mr. Marley said.

When Kevin left the church, it was already dark.
The burglars would be coming soon!

He ran all the way home.

Kevin made a plan that was full of booby traps.

He scattered toy cars

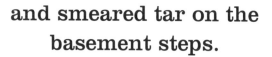
and smeared tar on the basement steps.

He made a big pile of feathers

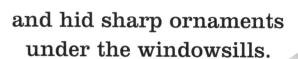
and hid sharp ornaments under the windowsills.

He sprayed water on
the front steps

and tied paint cans to ropes.

He stretched a trip wire
through the hallway

and built an escape route
to his tree house.

At nine o'clock, Marv and Harry returned to the McCallisters' house, ready to steal everything inside.

They didn't know that Kevin had sprayed water all over the steps…

...or that the water had frozen
into slick, slippery ice.

Marv and Harry slipped
on the toy cars

and were knocked over
by paint cans.

Kevin escaped through
his bedroom window

and ran next door to his
neighbor's house.

Unfortunately, Marv and Harry
were close behind.

"Now we've got you, kid!"
Harry said.

Mr. Marley arrived just in time! **WHACK! WHACK!**
He bonked the burglars with his snow shovel
and called the police.

Then he brought Kevin home.

That night, Kevin left a note
for Santa Claus, along with
some milk and cookies.

He couldn't wait for
Christmas morning.

Dear Santa,
I don't need
any presents.
Just bring back
my family.
Love,
Kevin McCallister

When he woke up the next day,
Kevin rushed into the living room.
"Mom? Dad? Is anyone here?"

No one answered him.

Dear Santa,
I don't need
any presents.
Just bring back
my family.
Love,
Kevin McCallister

Then he heard a familiar voice.

"Kevin? Is that you?"

His mother was home!

"I missed you so much,"
he said, giving her a giant hug.

"I missed you, too," she said.

"Where are the others?"
Kevin asked.

The front door flew open, and
there they were! His father, his brothers and
sisters—everybody was home at last.

"Are you okay?" his father asked.

"I'm just happy you're all back," Kevin said.
"Merry Christmas!"